Clifford
Goes to the Doctor

For Jillian

The author would like to thank Grace Maccarone and Frank Rocco for their contributions to this book.

Library of Congress Cataloging-in-Publication Data
Bridwell, Norman.
Clifford goes to the doctor / by Norman Bridwell.
p. cm.
Summary: Clifford the big red dog visits his veterinarian, Dr. Smart,
who has given him a check-up every year since he was almost too small to be weighed.
ISBN 978-0-545-23142-8 (pbk.)
[1. Veterinary medicine--Fiction. 2. Dogs--Fiction.] I. Title.
PZ7.B7633Cjim 2011
[E]--dc22
2010016768

ISBN 978-0-545-23142-8
10 9 8 7 6 5 4 3   11 12 13 14 15/0
Printed in the U.S.A. 40
First edition, June 2011

SCHOLASTIC READER
LEVEL 1
50-250 WORDS

Clifford
Goes to the Doctor

Norman Bridwell

Cartwheel
·B·O·O·K·S·®

SCHOLASTIC INC.
New York   Toronto   London   Auckland
Sydney   Mexico City   New Delhi   Hong Kong

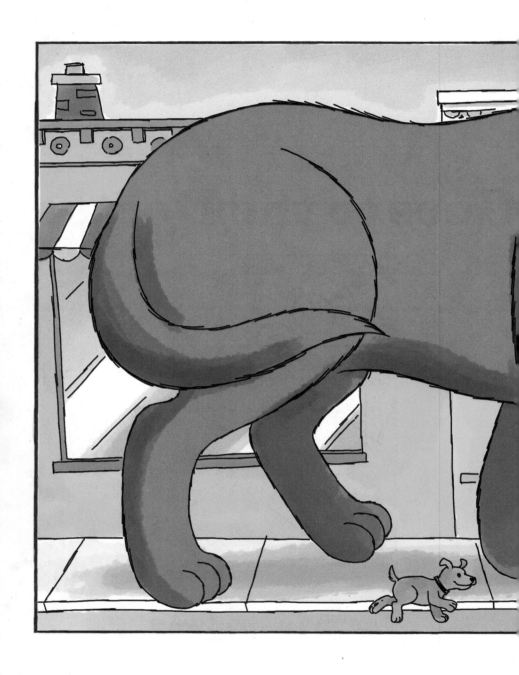

Every year, Clifford visits Dr. Smart.

The first year, Clifford
was very small.

He was the smallest pet
in the waiting room.

Clifford liked Dr. Smart right away.

She helped him onto her table.

She turned around and then
Clifford was gone.

He was hiding in her pocket!

Clifford was so small Dr. Smart
weighed him on a postage scale.

She measured him with a ruler.

She looked at his eyes,
ears, and mouth.

Then Dr. Smart gave Clifford a shot.

Clifford didn't like the shot,
but he was very brave.

"Clifford is healthy," Dr. Smart said,
"but he is very small."

One year later, Clifford went back.
Dr. Smart was surprised to see him.

Clifford couldn't fit in the doorway!

"I will give Clifford his checkup outside,"
Dr. Smart said.

The nurses got a scale to weigh
Clifford, but he was too big.

Dr. Smart had a smart idea.
Her friend had a truck.

They drove on the highway.

They stopped at a weigh station.

Clifford got on the scale.
"He is a good weight," said Dr. Smart.

Dr. Smart checked Clifford's heartbeat.

"Sounds good," she said.

She looked in Clifford's eyes and ears.

And she looked in Clifford's mouth.
"Everything is good," said Dr. Smart.

It was time for Clifford's shot.
Clifford still didn't like shots.

"You are very brave," Dr. Smart said.
Then she gave him a treat.

Clifford's checkup was done.

"Clifford, you are healthy," Dr. Smart said.

"You can stop growing now." And he did.